A FRIEND AT THE ZOO

By Mary Tillworth

Based on the screenplay "The Lonely Rhino" by Michael Rubiner, Bob Mittenthal,
Robert Scull, Johnny Belt, and Clark Stubbs

Based on the TV series *Bubble Guppies,* created by Robert Scull and Jonny Belt

Cover illustrated by Sue DiCicco

Cover illustration colored by Gary Hunt

Interior illustrated by Paul E. Nunn

A Random House PICTUREBACK® Book

Random House  New York

randomhouse.com/kids
ISBN: 978-0-449-81389-8
Printed in the United States of America
10 9 8 7 6

One beautiful summer day, Gil and Molly were playing with a flying disc. As Molly threw the disc to Gil, a gust of wind carried it over a high wall.

So Gil and Molly went to get it back.

On the other side of the wall, they found a zoo! Gil and Molly saw their disc next to the zookeeper. The zookeeper was feeding a large animal with a horn on its nose.

"Meet Monty the Rhino," said the zookeeper.
"He looks kinda sad," said Gil.
The zookeeper nodded. "I think Monty's a little lonely.
He could use a friend."

"I'll be his friend!" said Gil.
"Me too!" said Molly.
The zookeeper smiled. "Thank you so much. But I think Monty needs a friend that can live with him at the zoo."

Gil and Molly said goodbye to Monty and the zookeeper and headed to school.

"I'm gonna find a friend for Monty that can live at the zoo," said Gil.

Molly smiled. "Good idea! Let's go tell Mr. Grouper!"

Molly and Gil swam to class. Together with Goby, Deema, Oona, and Nonny, they greeted their teacher. "Good morning, Mr. Grouper!"

"Good morning, class!" Mr. Grouper replied.

"Gil and I saw a lonely rhino named Monty at the zoo,"
said Molly. "Mr. Grouper, will you help us find him a friend?"
"Sure!" replied Mr. Grouper. "Let's go to the zoo and find
a friend for Monty. Line up, everybody!"

At the zoo, the Bubble Guppies saw many animals in their habitats. "A habitat is a place where an animal lives," said Nonny. The animals lived in lots of different habitats. Monkeys swung from vines in the jungle. A panda climbed over his bamboo house. The penguins stayed nice and cool in their icy igloo.

Nonny pointed to a sign with a picture of a bird on the horn of a rhino. "Look," he said. "This bird and the rhino are friends."

"Maybe Monty should have a bird friend!" said Gil.

"That's a great idea!" said the zookeeper.

"We have lots of birds at the zoo!" said the zookeeper. "We just have to find a bird who can live in the same habitat as Monty."

The zookeeper pointed to a penguin. "Do you think a penguin would be a good friend?"

"No. A penguin needs a cold place to live, and Monty lives in a warm place!" said Molly.

"What about a macaw?" asked the zookeeper. "He lives in a tropical forest, where it's warm."

Gil shook his head. "A macaw lives high up in the trees, but rhinos live in flat, grassy plains. He wouldn't make a good friend for Monty."

"I have just the bird!" said the zookeeper. She brought out a small brown bird. "This is a tickbird. He lives in the warm grasslands."

"Just like Monty!" said Molly.

"It's like the bird from the sign," said Gil. "A tickbird is the perfect bird friend for Monty!"

"Monty, meet your new friend!" said the zookeeper.
The tickbird flew over and landed on Monty's horn.
Monty started to smile.
"Hooray!" cheered the Bubble Guppies.

"Thanks for visiting the zoo today," the zookeeper told Molly and Gil.

Molly laughed. "It was wonderful! We learned so much about animals—and we found the perfect friend for Monty!"